One Hockey Night

David Ward

illustrations by
Brian Deines

North Winds Press
An Imprint of Scholastic Canada Ltd.

The illustrations in this book were created in oil on canvas. The illustrator wishes to thank the Saunderson-Werker and Stevenson-Lee families for the great poses.

The text type was set in 16 point Poppl-Pontifex Regular.

Library and Archives Canada Cataloguing in Publication

Ward, David, 1967-
One hockey night / David Ward ; illustrations by Brian Deines.

ISBN 978-0-545-98995-4

I. Deines, Brian II. Title.

PS8595.A69H623 2010   jC813'.6   C2010-900933-9

6 5 4 3 2 1   Printed in Singapore 46   10 11 12 13 14

Author's Note

My earliest memories of hockey are of skating outdoors at night in Dollard-des-Ormeaux, the town where I lived. I remember the cold, and the shadowy shapes of neighbours gliding in and out of the darkness. Behind our home was farmland, which was somewhat swampy in the spring, and where natural rinks would form in the freezing winters. Pond hockey was a part of winter life in Quebec.

Eventually the family moved to British Columbia, and I discovered that outdoor rinks and outdoor hockey were an important part of life throughout Canada.

Many years later, I came across a *Hockey Night in Canada* contest for the best backyard rink. One of the contestants was from Little Harbour, Nova Scotia. Ingeniously, he had made a rink from lobster crates. How Canadian! Inspired, I felt that this gem of Canadian hockey history could be the basis of a story. And as *One Hockey Night* was taking shape, another small Nova Scotia town made big hockey news. Sidney Crosby, from Cole Harbour, became the youngest NHL captain ever to hold aloft the Stanley Cup.

Since writing my first hockey picture book, *The Hockey Tree,* I have met thousands of Canadians who have told me their own hockey stories. May the games and the stories continue.

Owen watched the falling snow from his bedroom window. Two weeks ago, the family had moved to Nova Scotia from the other side of the country. There were still boxes to unpack. It was almost Christmas, and all his friends were far away in Saskatchewan. Worse still, there was no frozen lake here in Kettle Harbour. How could he and his sister play hockey the way they loved best?

"Owen!" Holly called. "Come and take shots on me."

Owen sighed and trudged downstairs. He grabbed his jacket and pulled on his boots and gloves. Then he took his hockey stick from the coat rack.

His sister picked up her goalie mask. "Three goals . . . then I'll shoot on you."

They went out the front. The backyard was off limits. "It'll just be for a while," Dad had said. "Sort of a secret."

It had been snowing for hours. The road wasn't plowed yet, but together they shovelled the driveway. Owen dragged the net into position and Holly got ready.

Holly was a good goalie. When she wore her big pads, Owen had to try his hardest to score. After several shots he finally beat her on her glove-hand side.

"I wish we were playing on the lake," he shouted. "And I miss our friends."

Holly's helmet bobbed up and down. "Me too."

Only a few days till Christmas, and nothing felt the same.

9

After dinner the doorbell rang. Owen and Holly raced to the front hall. A neighbour, Mrs. Penner, stood on the porch, her face glowing from the cold. A boy hung back on the bottom step. "We've brought the lobster crates your dad asked for," she said. "And C.J. wanted to say hello. You've met him at school, right, Owen?"

Owen looked at him and said, "Maybe you can come over and play shinny in the driveway sometime."

C.J. smiled and nodded.

At that moment, Mom took over. She shooed Owen and Holly toward the living room and closed the door behind her. They could hear the adults' muffled voices on the porch and a hoot from C.J.

Owen and Holly exchanged glances. What was this all about?

The next evening Owen was reading in the living room when he saw two men walk up the driveway carrying lobster crates. They disappeared into the garage. Owen got up to check things out, but right then his mother called, "Would you help Holly with her homework, please?"

"I just want to see what Dad's doing," Owen said.

"Wait a little longer, dear," she said. "You'll find out soon."

Later, Holly came into Owen's room. "Something is going on," she said. "Dad's been in the garage a lot."

She looked wistfully out the window. "I like my new pads. And I like taking shots out front. But nothing's as good as playing hockey on the lake with our friends. I wish we were back home."

"I know," Owen agreed. "The driveway isn't the same. I want to get my skates on and play a real game on ice!" His shoulders slumped. "Maybe nobody plays hockey around here."

On Christmas Eve the table was set with red candles and napkins for the next day. The tree, and the presents beneath it, glittered invitingly. Everything looked familiar, but something was missing.

"I wish we were still at our old place," Owen said. "Holly and I miss skating on the lake."

Their parents looked at one another. "We know you do," said Mom.

"And tonight we have a surprise," Dad added.

Holly looked up. "We're going back?" she asked hopefully.

"No . . ." said Dad. "We're going out! Get your skates, you two. And your sticks and gloves."

"But it's Christmas Eve!" cried Owen.

"Yes, it is!" Mom laughed.

Mystified, Owen and Holly collected their equipment and made for the front door.

"Not that way," said Mom. She pointed to the back door. "That way. Through the backyard."

Dad had already disappeared.

Following their mom, they trudged to the back of the property.

21

Past the hedge, Owen sucked in a breath
of astonishment. Bright lights twinkled in the
trees, lighting up a glimmering expanse of ice.
Dad stood at the centre, leaning on his shovel.
A wall of lobster crates surrounded the ice.

"A hockey rink!" Owen and Holly shouted.
"Merry Christmas!" chorused their parents.

Neighbours began to arrive, one by one, through the hedge, with skates slung over their shoulders. Mrs. Penner wore an Edmonton Oilers jersey and C.J. was waving his hockey stick. Owen waved back. A host of colourful jerseys paraded through the falling snow — Montreal, Toronto, Calgary, Ottawa, Vancouver.

Owen's father grinned. "Ready?" he asked.
He tossed a puck onto the rink.

The cold air and the slap of sticks on the ice made Owen feel as though he were back on the lake in Saskatchewan. This is the best, he thought, as Holly made a save off C.J.

"Owen!" she called, and held out the puck as he skated by.

"C'mon, C.J.!" he shouted, and passed the puck to his new friend. "It's hockey night in Kettle Harbour!"